WE CAN JUMP

By Barbara Williams

Illustrated by Mary P. Maloney and Stan Fleming

CHILDRENS PRESS, CHICAGO

Library of Congress Cataloging in Publication Data

Williams, Barbara.
We can jump.

SUMMARY: An easy-to-read invitation to jump in a variety of ways.
[1. Play—Fiction] I. Mallone, Mary, illus.
II. Fleming, Stanley, illus. III. Title.
PZ7.W65587We [E] 72-8346
ISBN 0-516-03664-5

Printed in the United States of America.

4 5 6 7 8 9 10 11 12 13 14 15 16 17 18 19 20 21 22 23 24 25 R 75 74

WE CAN JUMP

Jump. Jump.

"See me jump."

Jump up.

Jump
down.

“I like to jump.”

“Do you like to jump?”

"Yes. Yes. I like to jump."

Jump in.

Jump on.

Jump on and on and on.

“We can jump.
Here we go.”

"Hello."
"Hello."

"See us jump."

“I can jump.
See me jump.”

"This is fun.
Here we go."

"Hello."

"Hello."

"See us jump."

"Mother can jump.
See Mother and me
jump."

“This is fun.”

"Can you jump?"
"Yes. I can jump."

“This is fun.”

"Here we go."

"Can you jump?"

"No. I do not
want to jump."

"I can ride."

“See the car go.”

"Oh! Oh! See us jump!"

No one can jump.

About the Author: Barbara Williams has been writing since she was old enough to hold a pencil and publishing since she was in grade school. In addition to *We Can Jump,* she has had twelve books, three plays, and a number of magazine stories, poems, and articles published. Her writing covers a wide range of interests—from childrens' picture books to college textbooks—but she is happiest when working on something whimsical. Mrs. Williams now lives in Salt Lake City with her husband and children. She loves to travel with her family, especially to places of historical interest.

About the Artists: Mary Maloney was born in Chicago. She received her Bachelor of Fine Arts from Northern Illinois University in 1970. A year of travel followed which included Europe, North Africa, Iceland and Israel. Mary took a great many photographs during that year, particularly of young people. She came to believe that "the essence of a country can be found in the faces of its children" through their openness and curiosity. One of Mary's many outside interests include getting out into the land and "rediscovering America".

Stan Fleming was born in Medicine Hat, Alberta, Canada. After his high school graduation in Canada he secured a scholarship at the school of Fine Arts at the University of Alberta. He also graduated from the Art Institute of Chicago. He opened his own art and photography studio in Chicago in 1952 and since then his work has appeared in innumerable books and magazines.